Kitty
in
High School

Kitty in the Middle
Kitty in the Summer
Only Jody
Back Yard Angel

Kitty
in
High School

Judy Delton

Houghton Mifflin Company
Boston

Library of Congress Cataloging in Publication Data

Delton, Judy.
  Kitty in high school.

  Summary: Just after World War II, Kitty becomes a
freshman at a Catholic high school in St. Paul, where she
reevaluates her friendships and turns her attention to
boys.
  [1. Catholic high schools—Fiction.   2. High schools—
Fiction.   3. Schools—Fiction.   4. Friendship—Fiction]
I. Title.
PZ7.D388Kg 1984   [Fic]   84–523
ISBN 0–395–35334–3

Printed in the United States of America

S   10   9   8   7   6   5   4   3   2

For Kathleen Holmberg,
who remembers SJA

Contents

Kitty
in
High School

1
An Unexpected Vacation

"Polio," said Kitty in disgust, as she caught a maple leaf that drifted into the rowboat. "The one year I looked forward to starting school. Our first year in high school and there has to be an epidemic."

Kitty was upset every time she thought about it. Why couldn't there have been an epidemic when she was in eighth grade with Sister Lucia, who gave three hours of homework each day? And there had been no epidemic the year she was going into fourth grade with Sister Ursuline, who rapped people on the head with her ruler when they couldn't find the "do" in do-re-mi.

But now, when she was finally going to be a

real freshman, the schools weren't even going to open. So here it was September, and Kitty and her friends Margaret Mary and Eileen were on a boat in the middle of Big Lake. To avoid contamination, people had been advised to stay out of crowds during the hot summer months, and Eileen's parents had invited Kitty and Margaret Mary to their lakeside cottage.

Kitty's parents were relieved that she would be safely out of the city until the danger had passed. Ever since Thomas O'Keefe, a classmate of Kitty's, had died of polio earlier that year, her mother had worried terribly about the epidemic. Whenever Kitty had a cold or a sniffle, her mother would rush her off to the doctor to make sure it wasn't polio. The scariest things to have were a fever or a stiff neck. Kitty was always sure she had a stiff neck, but it was a well-known fact that if you had a stiff neck and could still touch your chin to your chest, you didn't have polio. Kitty tried it right now, sitting in the rowboat. She was safe. Her chin could touch her chest.

Eileen was rowing the boat. Margaret Mary was busy knitting a pair of mittens to give to her sister for Christmas. Kitty watched her. Margaret Mary always looked neat and clean, even when she was on vacation. Kitty couldn't understand how she managed to keep her anklets white and clean in a dirty boat. Kitty never wore anklets at the lake.

Looking at Margaret Mary, Kitty wondered what it would be like to have a sister. She couldn't imagine anyone else besides her mother and her father and her in their small house on Jefferson Avenue in St. Paul. Her whole life seemed to involve groups of three. Three in her family, three in her group of friends. It would be fun to be able to say, "My sister is going to college," or "I have to take care of my little brothers this morning."

Kitty and Eileen were both only children, but Margaret Mary had three sisters and a brother. Margaret Mary was very mature for her age, everyone said. Back in grammar school, Father Bliss had once called her the perfect St. Anthony's student. As the oldest of five children, Margaret Mary had a lot of responsibilities at home. She could cook and iron, and when she led the family rosary she knew all the Mysteries, even the Glorious. Kitty never had to cook or clean, and she didn't know any of the mysteries of the rosary, either. Still, Kitty liked Margaret Mary. She was safe to be with. Kitty never had to worry that Margaret Mary would get her into trouble.

Eileen dropped the anchor in the water with a splash.

"It feels wicked, not being in school in September," said Margaret Mary. Surprised, the two girls looked at her. How could Margaret Mary know what it felt like to be wicked? "Well, of course, it's not our fault," she added quickly. "But it is the first September we haven't been wearing uniforms and doing homework."

"I hope it never opens," said Eileen dreamily, trailing her fingers in the water. For as long as Kitty had known her, Eileen had always looked forward to being grown up and going to New York and even to Europe. She wasn't as excited as her two friends were for school to begin.

"We're going to have a good time at St. Joan's," said Margaret Mary. "We're lucky to be going there, to have a good Catholic education. Lots of girls don't have those advantages."

"Pooh," said Eileen. "I don't know about advantages, but it'll be fun to wear lipstick and have boyfriends."

"There are no boys at St. Joan's," Kitty reminded her. Kitty had had a bad experience with a boy in fourth grade and didn't know if she was ready to chance liking another one.

"St. Joan's girls date St. Francis and St. Thomas boys," said Eileen, who knew more about these things than the other two.

"My mother says we're too young to have boys on our minds," said Margaret Mary.

"No, we're not," said Eileen. She didn't mind taking issue with Margaret Mary's mother, especially when she wasn't there. "Once we're in high school we're practically grown up."

Kitty shivered at the thought of boyfriends and dating and dances. If nothing else, high school would surely be a change from St. Anthony's.

Eileen reached casually into her sweater pocket. She took out a gold tube with simulated pearls on the sides. Then she pulled it apart and turned a knob on the bottom of one end.

"Look," she said, holding it up in the sun.

"What in the world is it?" said Margaret Mary.

"Eileen!" said Kitty. "Where did you get lipstick?"

"My mom bought it for me," said Eileen. "It's called Cyclamen Evening. Isn't it pretty?"

Spellbound, the girls watched Eileen apply the bluish pink make-up to her lips. Then she rubbed her lips together and blotted them with a tissue.

"Your *mother* gave it to you?" said Margaret Mary, horrified at the notion.

Eileen nodded. "She says I can wear it when I dress up and go out."

The girls looked at Eileen's smooth, bright pink lips.

"Can I put some on?" asked Kitty.

Eileen handed her the tube. With no mirror, Kitty looked over the side of the boat into the water and tried to apply the lipstick. How did Eileen get it on so evenly, wondered Kitty. The tube seemed to slide up and down with the motion of the boat. She remembered watching older girls outline their lips — quickly, expertly — and then rub the two together carefully.

With lipstick on her lips, Kitty felt like another person, someone she didn't know or even recognize. She imagined her arms and legs growing longer, slimmer, and she knew that when she got out of the boat, she would walk differently. Over the edge of the boat she could see her face in the clear water. She seemed older and could almost feel her body filling out where it had been straight before.

"Do you know what else?" said Eileen, breaking through Kitty's reverie. She took up the anchor and began to row to shore. "I'm getting high heels."

Margaret Mary's mouth grew thin, her lips pressed together in disapproval.

"Well, just patent leather pumps. But they have heels an inch high. I'll have to wear nylon stockings with them. And a garter belt that goes around my waist instead of over my shoulders."

Kitty felt a tingling in the bottom of her toes that went right up to her knees. She had always dreamed of the day she could wear high heels, but whenever she asked, her mother always told her she was much too young and not to get any ideas yet. And nylons! No one Kitty's age was allowed to wear nylons, and besides, they were considered a luxury because they were still scarce so soon after World War II, and they ran easily.

"My mother says you can't really be dressed up with oxfords, or even Mary Janes, at our age."

Kitty felt a wave of warmth for Eileen's mother. What an understanding, sensible woman.

"Of course, I'd only wear them on Sundays, and for parties," added Eileen. "Not for school or anything."

"You couldn't anyway," said Margaret Mary. "We have to wear uniform shoes at St. Joan's. They're serviceable and good for our feet."

"Who cares?" said Eileen.

"I hate oxfords." Kitty sighed.

There was silence in the boat as they pulled it into the dock. Margaret Mary's remarks had dampened some of the enthusiasm they had felt at the thought of high school, and for the first time in her memory, Kitty felt irritated with her old friend. But as she was getting out of the boat, she remembered the lipstick, and it brought back once again the feeling that changes were in store for her that year. She walked into the cottage feeling the magic of Cyclamen Evening. Even when the color wore off later that evening, the mood stayed with her and continued to warm her the rest of the night.

2
"Courtesy Counts"

The days at the lake sped by. The nights grew cool, and after supper the girls would put on sweaters when they went to buy the evening paper and a candy bar from Mrs. Martin.

Mrs. Martin ran the nearby resort and lodge. The girls frequently came upon her stirring a boiler full of white sheets on the stove, her thick legs anchored to a pair of tennis shoes with the sides cut out for her bunions. She smiled at the girls as she handed them the paper.

"I see the schools are opening next week in the Twin Cities," said Mrs. Martin one evening as September came to a close.

Kitty took the paper from her to look for

herself. Sure enough! There it was in print! St. Joan's Academy was among those listed as opening on Monday. Kitty jumped up and down in her excitement, and even Eileen looked relieved.

"I was afraid we would never be in high school," Margaret Mary said.

"So was I," said Kitty.

Eileen snorted.

Waving the paper in their hands, the girls ran back to the cottage, anxious to tell Eileen's parents the news. Eileen's parents were the kind of people Kitty always wished her parents were. Eileen's father joked with the girls and often brought his daughter presents. Her mother seemed younger than Kitty's mother and was more spirited. She let the girls drink grape juice in Eileen's room. Kitty's mother always worried that it would spill and stain something.

"We'll have to get packed!" Eileen's mother said when the girls rushed in with the news about the opening of school. "We can leave for home on Saturday morning."

During the ride home, the girls' heads were spinning with plans for the first day of school. Kitty's new green wool jumper and the white blouse with SJA embroidered on the collar were all ready, she knew. She had already gone with her mother to buy new brown leather oxfords, which she would wear with stockings of tan cotton or lisle.

"I hope I get into the glee club," Eileen was saying. "St. Joan's is famous for their glee club. They sing all over the Twin Cities."

Kitty wished she could sing well. She had never learned along with the others how to find "do," and she wasn't sure she could find it even now. The glee club probably wouldn't want anyone who didn't know where "do" was.

"I'm taking Latin," said Kitty.

"We all are," said Eileen. "It's required."

"I wanted to take two religion classes, but it

isn't allowed," said Margaret Mary. "Only seniors can."

Kitty and Eileen looked at each other and sighed. Kitty felt a twinge of annoyance with Margaret Mary again. Religion was like gym, something no one would take unless she had to. Margaret Mary probably likes volleyball too, thought Kitty, wishing she were good at sports. Playing softball or tennis might be good exercise. It wasn't that she couldn't run fast or hit balls. It was just that she never could get the rules straight. When they played neighborhood softball, no one wanted her on their side. Once she had run around the bases the wrong way and banged into a player on her own team. They were both called out, and her team lost the game.

"I wonder how many classes we'll be in together," said Margaret Mary. It was very important to the girls that they be together. "My mother says that we should meet new friends now that we are in high school. It's not good to be in a clique."

"What's a clique?" asked Kitty.

"It's a small group," said Eileen.

"Then we're a clique already," said Kitty.

"No," said Margaret Mary. "It's when you won't talk to anyone else or let anyone else in the group."

Kitty felt slightly guilty. She liked their group the way it was. They had fun together. Still, Margaret Mary could be awfully tiresome at times. She probably keeps us from getting into real trouble though, thought Kitty. Why, if she and Eileen didn't have someone to hold them down, there was no telling how far they might go. And Kitty wouldn't want any girls like Ruthie Cobza in her group, her and her boy-crazy friends.

By the time the girls got to the city, they had made plans to meet in the morning at the corner of Randolph and Albert, where they would get the streetcar to the academy.

When Kitty arrived at her house, her mother looked white and stiff and smooth — more so than Kitty remembered her. She reminded Kitty to take her shoes off at the door, and then hugged her.

Kitty's father kissed her. "Glad to have you home," he said. "It was quiet around here with you gone." Kitty's father was quiet himself, but he was always there when Kitty needed him. He was there when she needed to be hugged or needed a wall in her room painted dark green or needed help writing an essay with a surprise ending. Her father was good at surprise endings.

After eating a piece of her mother's home-made pie, Kitty went up to her room. She noticed with satisfaction that her school clothes were hanging on the door of her closet, just as they had always been when she was going to St. Anthony's. But this time it was a high school uniform that was waiting for her. Kitty was glad to be back home in her own little room, where she could be alone to think. Back with all her familiar things around her — the little white radio her father had bought her, the dressing table with the chintz skirt her mother had made. Even the smell of furniture polish and floor wax was reassuring. Kitty put all of the clothes from her suitcase down the laundry chute for her mother to wash and iron, even the ones that Eileen's mother had already washed at the lake. Her mother had stringent standards of cleanliness, and Kitty's clothes were always whiter and stiffer and smoother than anyone else's.

That night in her clean dark room, with smooth, ironed sheets against her skin, Kitty was suddenly afraid of going to high school. That surprised her. For a moment she almost wished she were going back to St. Anthony's, with its familiar faces, classrooms, and nuns. Even if the nuns were crabby, thought Kitty, you knew what to expect. There were no surprises.

Kitty scolded herself. That was exactly why she had wanted to go to St. Joan's. She wanted surprises in her life. She couldn't hang onto the same boring things forever, she had to grow up.

When she finally fell asleep, she dreamed that Eileen and Margaret Mary went to the public school at the last minute, leaving her all alone to face her new life at St. Joan's.

Morning came quickly and Kitty put on the strange, new green uniform with its long-sleeved white blouse. She ate a quick breakfast, kissed her mother and father, and left to become a freshman. "At last," breathed Kitty, as she got on the streetcar with the other green-uniformed girls going to St. Joan's. "At last I'm in high school!" Her new brown oxfords felt stiff, the way she imagined Dutch wooden clogs must be. Her white blouse with SJA on the collar was stiff too, from the starch her mother had put in it, and it scratched Kitty's arms. Kitty carried a brand new plaid book bag which was empty except for a pencil and blank notebook.

The three friends chattered away at each other as they rode through the dark Selby

Tunnel to the academy. But when they climbed down from the streetcar and were in front of the school, Kitty stopped and said, "I feel scared."

"Scared of what?" said Eileen, tossing her curls back. She never seemed to be afraid of anything. "Those ugly old nuns don't scare me. They're probably just like the crabby nuns at St. Anthony's."

"No, they're stricter," said Kitty. "And the school is bigger. We'll probably get lost changing rooms and everything every hour."

Eileen dismissed that with a wave of her hand. "C'mon, let's go inside," she said.

St. Joan's Academy was a massive old sandstone building erected in 1850. The school had been founded by nuns sent over from France. At first it was only a boarding school, but now there were so many people in St. Paul and Minneapolis that there were only two or three boarders from out of town. The rest of the students were girls from the Twin Cities.

The school had twelve-foot high ceilings,

large old windows that had to be opened using a window pole, and hollow-sounding wooden floors in the wide hallways. In one wing was a chapel and in another was the Jeanne D'Arc auditorium. In between the two wings was a small courtyard with a fish pond and a large statue of St. Joan with benches around it. The second and third floors of the building were the convent, where the nuns lived. It was definitely *private,* no students allowed.

As the friends entered the main door of the school, a tall nun was handing out blue booklets called "Courtesy Counts at SJA." She directed them through the courtyard to the auditorium. When all the students were assembled, another nun came out on the stage and introduced herself as Sister Chrysostom, the principal of the school.

"It sounds like a flower," whispered Kitty to Eileen.

Sister Chrysostom went on to explain how lucky the girls were to be freshmen at St. Joan's.

"That's what my mother says," whispered Margaret Mary.

Kitty was tired of hearing what Margaret Mary's mother said. Couldn't she think for herself?

Sister Crysostom told them what high standards they would be expected to live up to, and that the seams in their stockings were always to be straight, and that no one was to miss daily mass. Then she explained the honor roll system and stressed what a fine thing it was to wear a MAGNA CUM LAUDE button on one's uniform, which signified all A grades. For the students with a B average, there were the CUM LAUDE buttons. And, of course, everybody with lower grades wore no buttons at all.

"I'll bet you get to be magna cum laude every semester, Margaret Mary," said Kitty.

Margaret Mary blushed. "I hope so," she said.

"Now," said Sister Chrysostom, "open your little blue books called Courtesy Counts at SJA."

All the students opened their booklets. Sister Chrysostom read out loud as they followed along, explaining the points that needed explaining. She showed them how to clap their hands at public performances by tapping the fingertips of one hand lightly against the palm of the other, and not tapping palm against palm, which was unladylike.

In the classroom, she continued, feet were to be flat on the floor or crossed at the ankles. Legs were never to be crossed at the knees. In chapel they were to genuflect as a group and on both knees if the Blessed Sacrament was exposed. In greeting, or when saying "Pardon me," students were to use a nun's entire name. "Pardon me, *Sister* Chrysostom."

At meals one should never butter a whole piece of bread, forks should always be placed tines up, and soup spoons should be dipped away from and not toward one. At a formal tea, an afternoon dress should be worn, never a skirt and sweater. Also, gloves must be worn and a purse carried.

"I'm never going to remember all of this," whispered Kitty.

"It's dumb," said Eileen.

Ignoring Eileen, Margaret Mary turned to Kitty. "We did most of these things at St. Anthony's," she said, trying to reassure her.

Kitty sighed. It all sounded new to her. And it seemed like a lot of work. Although classes hadn't even begun yet, Kitty had used several pages of her notebook already, jotting down Sister's rules and suggestions. Margaret Mary knew all the rules already, Kitty supposed, and Eileen never intended to know or to follow them. Kitty was in the middle again, even here in high school.

"Now," said Sister Chrysostom, "we will learn the school song this morning." Two confident sophomores passed out sheets with the words and music on them. "We will use these copies this morning, but by tomorrow I'll expect each of you to have memorized the song," she added.

An upperclassman was at the piano and

played the melody briefly, as if she had done it many times. Kitty wondered if she would ever be an upperclassman and look so self-assured. It was hard to picture. There was so much to learn in high school that she imagined she could very well remain a freshman forever.

"Dear SJA," sang Sister, "No walls enclose thy spirit deep within . . . It lives in endless hearts, where ere our tenets have been."

Kitty liked the chorus: "School of happy memories, dear academy, let the ivy branches be a crown to thee. O guide of youth, dear SJA, grant us blessings day by day."

Everyone began to leave the auditorium humming "Dear SJA." Kitty frowned and repeated the words over and over to herself, trying to memorize them. She turned to her friends and saw that Margaret Mary was talking to one of the nuns. Eileen was walking out with a girl Kitty didn't recognize. Now Kitty didn't feel in the middle at all. She felt totally and miserably alone.

3
A New Friend

Mimi
Kitti Kitty
Kitti Kitti Kitti

"Who have you got for Latin?" said Eileen, running up to Kitty in the hall a few days after school opened. She was with a group of girls who were laughing and calling out Latin words to each other.

"Sister Sylvania."

"Oh, she's terrible I hear. We've got Sister Angelique. She's real young and she taught us 'Mairsy Doats' in Latin today! We even played a crossword game in Latin."

Kitty watched as Eileen went rushing off down the hall with her new companions, singing "Mares-eat-oats and does-eat-oats" in Latin. She felt betrayed. Sister Sylvania was terrible. She was old and strict and her face

25

had frown lines because she never smiled. She also gave four pages of homework every night and called her Katherine. "Katherine," she had said today, "conjugate the verb *love.*"

"Amo amas amat," sang Kitty. "Amamus amatis amant." Kitty had been up late the night before memorizing that with her father's help. High school was not all the fun she had thought it would be.

"We're lucky to have Sister Sylvania instead of Sister Angelique," said Margaret Mary, who had come up behind Kitty.

"My mother says we've learned more Latin in a few days than she learned in a year."

Kitty didn't care. Why in the world was it important how fast you learned Latin? What did it matter if you never learned it at all, in fact.

"Those girls with Eileen don't seem to be taking Latin seriously. We're lucky we aren't in their class."

Margaret Mary was beginning to sound like

a teacher, thought Kitty. Who wanted a teacher for a friend?

"I went ahead in the textbook last night, since I had finished the assignment," Margaret Mary was saying now. "Do you know what we have tomorrow? Listen: hic haec hoc, hi hae haec."

Kitty didn't want to hear what they would have tomorrow. Today was bad enough. "Love" was only one verb, there must be a million more to learn. And the present and past and perfect and past perfect with all their different endings were confusing. The nouns were even worse. The words "dative" and "accusative" and "ablative" were all jumbled together in Kitty's mind. She was sure she would not be able to get a passing grade in Latin, let alone ever see a CUM LAUDE button.

"Shut up, Margaret Mary. I don't want to hear any more Latin. I *hate* Latin."

Margaret Mary's mouth fell open. She looked shocked and hurt. Kitty's hand shot up to her mouth. What did I say, she thought, as she turned and ran up the staircase to her geometry class on the fourth floor. Still, to her surprise, she felt relieved she had said it!

Neither Eileen nor Margaret Mary had geometry with her, and that was a relief too. They both knew her too well. In geometry Kitty would be with girls who didn't know a thing about her. It was like having a whole new start. She could be anybody she wanted to be, someone completely different from the old Kitty at St. Anthony's. She was in high school now and had even worn lipstick once. She was not a child anymore.

Sister Cleone was assigning permanent seats. "Delores," she said, pointing to a seat in the row by the windows. "Then Kitty behind her."

Disappointed, Kitty walked over and took a seat behind Delores, who smiled at her, glad to see a familiar face. Kitty knew Delores from their days at St. Anthony's. She didn't smile back. She didn't want to sit near anyone she had known at St. Anthony's.

"And across the aisle from Kitty, Mimi."

Mimi. What a romantic name. It wasn't anything like a saint's name. Kitty turned to see what kind of girl would have the name Mimi. When she saw her, she decided instantly that she would like to be just like her. Mimi looked like a Mimi should look. Just to watch her was exciting! She was wearing lipstick, Kitty was pretty sure, even though it was too light for the nuns to see, and her regulation shoes were just a little bit nonregulation with a wedge heel instead of the standard rubber ones. They laced up like oxfords, but the wedge made them look 'hep.' Mimi's hair looked like it had a permanent wave, and when she stood up to pick up a holy card off the floor, Kitty noticed that her uniform fit a little more snugly than anyone else's. Not enough for Sister Chysostom to ask her to buy a larger size, just enough to accentuate the swing of her hips when she walked. When she leaned over toward her, Kitty could smell a scent that wasn't soap or baby powder. She was pretty sure it was perfume.

Sister Cleone had finished the seating arrangements and was drawing a figure on the blackboard. "This," she said, "is an isosceles triangle."

The girls took out their notebooks and settled down to draw and label the triangle.

"How do you spell isosceles?" asked Mimi.

Kitty looked up in surprise when she realized who was talking to her. This was her chance to get to know someone new. To *be* someone new! But who could she be?

"I don't know," said Kitty, trying to decide what kind of personality she should adopt while she had the chance.

Mimi laughed suddenly — a light, giggly laugh that started Kitty laughing, and pretty soon Sister Cleone glared at them from the front of the room. This felt dangerous, but

Kitty didn't care. It was fun. She didn't usually do dangerous things.

"Hey, what's your name?" whispered Mimi, snapping her gum as she spoke. Gum was definitely dangerous. Not only at St. Joan's, but at any school, even a public school. Kitty's mother never even let her chew gum at home.

"Kitty," said Kitty.

Mimi smiled again. "Cute."

Mimi thought her name was *cute!*

"I've got a sister named Fluffy," Mimi went on. "That's like Kitty, you know, soft and cuddly."

Kitty laughed again. Everything sounded funny now. Even Sister Cleone and her tangents. When the bell rang, Kitty realized she hadn't heard much of what Sister had said in class.

On the way home from school, Kitty tried to walk with a swing to her hips.

"What are you doing?" said Eileen. "Have you got something the matter with your leg?"

"No." Kitty frowned. "There's nothing wrong with my leg."

"You're sure grumpy."

"I'm not grumpy," snapped Kitty.

That evening, when Kitty sat down to do her geometry homework, she stared at the page in front of her for a long time, frowning. "What's a tangent?" she finally asked her father.

"You must have had that in class today," he said, "or it wouldn't be in your homework."

Kitty frowned and snapped the gum she had gotten from Mimi.

"Kitty," said her mother from the sink where she was washing the supper dishes. "Throw that gum away." Her mother was frowning too.

Kitty decided to skip the problem about the tangent and go on to the next one. It was about the number of degrees in the angles of an isosceles triangle. She couldn't remember hearing anything about angles.

"I can't do this stuff," she said.

"Why not?" said her father, who, while willing to help Kitty, was not willing to do her homework *for* her, as he always insisted. "You never had trouble with math before."

"I don't understand it."

"Did Sister talk about it today? What did she say?"

"I don't know . . . I'm not sure."

Her father looked surprised. "Maybe you had better pay more attention tomorrow," he said. "It seems like you haven't been listening very well in class lately."

The next day in class, Mimi passed Kitty a note. The handwriting was slanted and angular, and the i's in Mimi's signature were dotted with little hearts. The note said, "Why don't you come over to my house after school some afternoon? We've got a TV."

A television set! Kitty had never known anyone with a television set. Many people said that after the war TVs would be available to everyone, but as far as she knew, no one in St. Paul had one. If anyone in the United States

33

would have a television set, Kitty thought, Mimi would. Kitty wrote back that she would ask her mother and let her know tomorrow.

In her notebook, Kitty practiced writing in slanting letters like Mimi. She stopped copying down what Sister Cleone was putting on the board. I wish I had a name like Mimi, she said to herself. She wrote *Mimi* across the page. Then she wrote *Kitty* under it. Suddenly she decided to change the spelling of her name. She would spell it K-i-t-t-i. That would suit her new image. *Kitti,* she wrote up and down the page so that she'd get used to it.

The next morning, in the hallway between classes, Kitty told Mimi that her mother would allow her to go home on the streetcar with her. And later that day, Kitty handed in a Latin paper with her name spelled K-i-t-t-i at the top. Sister Sylvania asked her to remain after class and write her name correctly one hundred times. Smiling to herself, Kitty remained undaunted. She decided to keep the name *Kitti* except on Latin papers.

4
Wall-to-Wall
Carpeting

Mimi was the first person Kitty had ever met
who lived on the east side of St. Paul. Most
people who lived in Kitty's neighborhood
thought the east side was not the right sort of
place to live. People there wore their skirts a
little too short and lived in "modern" houses
built with green wartime lumber that shrank.
Kitty found it daring to be going to the home
of someone who lived on the east side.

When school was out for the day, Kitty told
Margaret Mary and Eileen that she wouldn't
be taking the Selby Lake streetcar with them.
Eileen was with some friends from her Latin
class. They were all shouting out long Latin

words to each other and laughing merrily. One of them had her arm around Eileen as though she were an old friend.

"That's okay," Eileen said.

"I'm going downtown, anyway," she added, as an afterthought.

"I'm going home with Mimi," said Kitty importantly.

"To the east side?" said Eileen, with scorn.

Margaret Mary looked worried. "We're at an age that is easily influenced by the company we keep," she said meaningfully, though she was careful not to say that Mimi was bad company. Margaret Mary was determined to forgive Kitty for her outburst the other day and pretend it had never happened. Just the same, she didn't want to risk being insulted again.

Kitty felt a twinge of guilt, as though she were deserting her lifelong friends. Still, a person couldn't stay the same all of her life. And Mimi was fun, even if she did live on the east side.

"I'll see you tomorrow morning at the car line," called Kitty, running to catch up with Mimi.

The two girls climbed on the Randolph Hazel Park streetcar. Once it got out of the downtown area, Kitty didn't recognize any part of the city they rode through. Now the car was riding on tracks through open fields. It was exciting to be riding the streetcar with Mimi. As they sat in the yellow cane seats, Mimi said, "Who is your boyfriend?"

"Boyfriend?" echoed Kitty. Since fourth grade she had been careful to avoid boys. "No one special," said Kitty carefully, sounding as casual as she could.

"I think this boy named Buzzy likes me," confided Mimi. "He lives on Maryland St. I'll show you his house sometime."

The mention of boyfriends started Kitty on a whole new train of thought. If Mimi had a boyfriend, then maybe she should have one too. After all, fourth grade was a long time ago, and boys probably became nicer as they grew older. They *seemed* nicer. It was high time she had a boyfriend. But where would she ever meet one? No boys her age lived in her neighborhood, and St. Joan's was an all-girls school. Her best chance to meet one was at the St. Thomas mixers, but they were held only once a month, and the first one wasn't until the end of December. She would need a boyfriend long before that, Kitty suspected, if she wanted to remain friends with Mimi. She wondered what Margaret Mary would say if she did manage to find a boyfriend. (Kitty already had a good idea what Margaret Mary's mother would think about that.)

"Mimi," said Kitty, turning to her in a burst of confidence. "I've got these friends from grade school, and they really are starting to bore me. They don't *do* anything. I mean, we never have any fun anymore."

Mimi put a piece of gum in her mouth and offered Kitty one. Kitty took it and thanked her. She felt very close to Mimi today.

"You mean Margaret Mary and Eileen?"

Kitty was surprised. She didn't know Mimi kept track of her friends. She nodded.

"That Margaret Mary is really a prude," Mimi said.

"Well, she *used* to be fun . . ." said Kitty. She didn't mind saying something about Margaret Mary herself, but it didn't seem right when Mimi agreed with her.

"Yeah, when you were kids," said Mimi. "But let's face it, we're freshmen now."

"Exactly!" said Kitty, feeling friendlier toward Mimi by the minute. "And every time I want to do anything fun and grown-up, she thinks it's wrong. Or her mother thinks it's wrong. 'My *mother* says we're too young' or 'My *mother* says that isn't good for us.' " Kitty spoke in mincing tones, imitating Margaret Mary.

Mimi laughed. "She'd bore me too. I outgrew all my childhood friends a long time ago." Mimi took out a comb and began running it casually through her hair. Kitty thought fleetingly of Sister Chrysostom's warning about not doing private things in public places. How daring Mimi was! Of course she would have outgrown her childhood friends. While Kitty, on the other hand, had the very same friends that she'd had in second grade. She never asked herself if she liked them or not, they were always just there.

The streetcar had left the open fields behind and was now back in the city again. When the conductor called "Ruth Street," Mimi pressed the button. The girls got off and walked down a street bordered on both sides by small trim bungalows that all had a similar modern look about them. They were the green lumber houses Kitty had heard about.

A girl passed them and said "hi" to Mimi. She had a short skirt and lots of powder and rouge on her face.

"Did you see her?" whispered Mimi when they'd passed. "That's Mickey Stransky. She's fast," she confided. Mimi looked into Kitty's puzzled face. "I mean with boys. Of course, she's seventeen. She goes to Wilson High."

Kitty had known there were girls like this, but she had never come so close to meeting one. She turned around to get another look at Mickey Stransky.

"How do you know?" asked Kitty.

"She doubles with a friend of mine. And my friend told me what goes on in the rumble seat when they double date." Mimi rolled her eyes up as she said this.

Kitty wanted to ask Mimi exactly what went on in the rumble seat, but now they had come to Mimi's house, and Mimi was busy taking the mail out of the box and searching through her purse for the key. Finding it at last, she unlocked the front door, and Kitty stepped into a living room that was unlike any she had ever seen. The furniture was plain and, of all things, blond, almost white. Blond end tables, blond chairs, a blond dining-room table. And on the floor was what Kitty knew must be a "wall-to-wall" carpet. In Kitty's house they had a large, old mahogany dining-room table with ornate legs, and a dark brown mohair davenport and chair in the living room. On the floors in both rooms Kitty's mother and father had laid rugs with designs along the borders. Nowhere had Kitty seen blond furniture, except in the movies. Margaret Mary's furniture was even older than Kitty's, and in her house the lamp shades had old-fashioned fringes. Eileen's parents had maple furniture everywhere, even in Eileen's room, and an Early American rug in front of the fireplace. Kitty imagined that all the houses in Hollywood must look like Mimi's, with blond furniture and wall-to-wall carpeting.

The house was very quiet. Nobody seemed to be around. The clock was ticking loudly. "We've got a new washing machine," said Mimi. "Come and see it."

Kitty followed Mimi to the basement. Sure enough, there it was, a machine that washed clothes all by itself, like a robot.

"It washes and rinses and we don't even have to put clothes through a wringer or anything," said Mimi proudly. "Even my dad can run it."

No matter how hard she tried, Kitty could not picture a father washing clothes. Mimi ran her hand over the washing machine.

"My mom says no machine can get clothes really clean. You have to boil them," said Kitty.

"This one does," said Mimi.

Although Kitty was still doubtful, she was certainly impressed.

"C'mon up to my room," said Mimi.

Kitty looked carefully at everything on the way so she would not forget anything. Mimi's room was even more of a surprise than the other rooms had been. It was definitely a grown-up room. Mimi had a dressing table with a satin skirt around it. The mirror over it was in the shape of a heart, just like the dots on her i's. And her furniture was blond, just as blond as the furniture in the living room. It was a real Hollywood bedroom.

"I'll just get this uniform off. I hate the thing, don't you?"

Kitty had never had any particular feeling about her uniform one way or the other. She had worn a uniform to school all of her life. But now she looked down at it anew. Uniforms made everyone the same, she thought. And what she wanted most was to be different. At least, different from her old self.

"Yeah, I hate it," she agreed.

Kitty suddenly wondered where Mimi's mother was. "Where's your mother?" she asked.

Mimi had her uniform halfway over her head. "At work," sounded a muffled voice.

Kitty had never met a mother who worked. "Does she work in the war plant?" she asked. She had an aunt who worked in the arms plant in New Brighton. But, of course, her aunt wasn't married.

"No, at Acme Insurance Company," said Mimi. "She's a secretary." Kitty tried to imagine having a secretary for a mother, but she couldn't.

"Who gets your supper?" she asked.

"We do. Me, or my sister Fluffy, or my dad."

Mimi had mentioned her father twice. It was a relief to know she had one. But a father getting a meal? Poor Mimi. How awful it must be to come home to an empty house with no one to fix snacks the way her own mother did.

"Now," said Mimi, "do you want to borrow my lipstick? It's Russian Sable, Elizabeth Arden's newest shade."

Kitty looked at the tube. The lip make-up being revealed as Mimi twisted the knob on the bottom was so dark it was almost black. She did not remember ever having seen Mimi wear it. Kitty was tempted.

"I wear Cyclamen Evening," she said reluctantly after a moment's hesitation. If she were to go home with traces of Russian Sable on her lips, her mother would probably never let her go to Mimi's again.

"O.K." said Mimi, applying a coat to her own lips and then rubbing them together with purpose. "Let's go watch TV now," she said, walking out into the living room in her slip.

Apparently Mimi had forgotten to put a dress on, or maybe that was part of living in a house made of green lumber — sitting in the living room in your underwear. But wasn't she nervous, Kitty wondered. Suppose a delivery man should come to the door.

The girls sat down on what Mimi referred to as a love seat, and Mimi opened the doors of a large blond cabinet. Inside was a round glass window. "Ready?" Mimi said, and then she pulled down all the shades in the room. She turned a knob on the face of the cabinet. After a while a low whine could be heard, and then a dot appeared in the middle of the window. The dot lengthened to a long line across what

Mimi called the screen. (Just like in the movies!) Then it widened into white light. Mimi looked at her watch.

"In ten minutes," she said, "the test pattern comes on. I'll get us some apples and stuff."

While she was gone, Kitty sat spellbound, watching the white lit screen. It was amazing to her that simply by turning a knob, a person could cause a white light to appear, or, better yet, see an actual picture of something going on somewhere else in the world. In a few minutes the test pattern would begin. Wait until she told Eileen and Margaret Mary about this. Mimi came back and they ate their apples silently as they watched the screen.

"It's four o'clock," said Mimi. "It'll be starting any second now."

Sure enough, the next moment a voice from inside the cabinet, just like from a radio, announced, "Good afternoon, ladies and gentlemen. Station KSTP will now present the test pattern for one half hour." Kitty watched closely, sitting on the edge of the love seat, while dots and dashes and lines came into view — a miracle of modern technology.

"I can't believe it!" said Kitty. "A real television set!"

"A comedy show comes on at five o'clock," said Mimi. "It's not too clear, and you can't hear the words, but it's funny."

Kitty was sorry she had to be on her way home by five o'clock. "The test pattern is fine," she said, settling back to watch it until she had to leave. After all, blond furniture, a mother who worked, and a live test pattern were enough for one day.

After the test pattern was over, Kitty said goodbye to her new friend. Riding the streetcar home, she thought about her exciting day. She thought about friends. A wave of guilt came over her for telling Mimi that Margaret Mary was boring. It might be true, Margaret Mary might be boring, but Kitty felt a stab of pain at betraying an old friend.

5
Luring Boys

"I don't believe it," said Eileen the next morning as the three girls were waiting for the streetcar.

"No one has a television set in their *house.*"

"It's true," said Kitty. She described the test pattern to Eileen and Margaret Mary, who both listened doubtfully.

"How could it come right into someone's living room?" asked Margaret Mary.

"Well it did," said Kitty. "I saw it."

They remained skeptical.

Over the next weeks, Kitty spent several afternoons at Mimi's house, and sometimes Mimi came to hers. Mimi introduced Kitty to new experiences — things she'd never done with Margaret Mary or Eileen. One of them was "luring boys."

"That's how you get a boyfriend," Mimi said. "You have to lure them. That's how everyone gets boyfriends."

"Really?" said Kitty, looking at Mimi with some consternation. She wondered if Mimi could have known just how much this very thing had been on her mind lately. "I thought you just met boys and got to be friends with them because you liked the same things."

Mimi shook her head vigorously. "Heck, no," she said. "You lure them."

Mimi showed Kitty how to comb her hair over one eye like Veronica Lake, the movie star, and how to curl the ends so they turned under in a page-boy style. Kitty's hair didn't want to go over one eye or turn under, so they used Mimi's mother's curling iron until it did. And each afternoon, when they got to Mimi's house, they would shed their green uniforms, and Mimi would lend Kitty a rabbit's hair pullover and some open-toed high-heeled shoes. All this was necessary for luring boys, Mimi insisted. Then they would saunter by Buzzy's house in a matter-of-fact way that was meant to look as if they were just out for a stroll and happened to be there accidentally.

"What if he sees us and comes out?" said Kitty nervously one afternoon.

"That's what we want," said Mimi. "So far he hasn't come out, but one of these days he'll be on his porch."

That prospect both thrilled and frightened Kitty.

And then one day, after Kitty and Mimi had gone to the corner of Buzzy's block five times, they finally saw him in front of his house, sitting on his porch swing.

"There he is!" said Mimi. "And there's another boy with him." Mimi patted her sweater down and straightened the seams of her stockings. "Now just look casual."

She pretended to be deep in conversation

with Kitty and slowed down right in front of Buzzy's house, just when Kitty was the most nervous.

"Well," she said in a loud voice. "I just can't make up my mind who to go to the prom with. Did you decide yet Kitty?"

Then Mimi, the daring, sat right down on Buzzy's front cement steps as if to rest a bit. Kitty wanted to run as fast as she could for Mimi's house, or better yet, her own.

"Hi," said a voice from the porch. "Is that you, Mimi?"

Shading her eyes with her hand, Mimi turned around from the step she was sitting on and looked up. "Well, for goodness sake, do *you* live here, Buzzy? Kitty, look who lives here, Buzzy McKenzie! Buzzy, this is my friend Kitty from St. Joan's."

"Hi," said Kitty.

"Hi," said Buzzy. "This is Skip." He jerked his head toward the other boy on the porch swing. Skip said "Hi."

After that there didn't seem to be anything

further to say. The boys sat on the porch in silence, swinging back and forth, and Kitty and Mimi sat on the cement steps in silence. Kitty wondered what the next step in "luring boys" was. It seemed a little dull now. She couldn't imagine why she'd been so nervous.

"We were walking to the root beer stand," said Mimi. "Do you want to come?"

Now Kitty felt nervous again. Where did Mimi get so much courage? If this is what it took to lure boys, she was doomed to be an old maid.

Buzzy shrugged his shoulders. "Want to?" he said to Skip.

"I've got to be home by five o'clock to take care of my little brother."

Kitty looked at Skip with sudden interest. Here was a boy who took care of his family. She pictured Skip feeding his little brother and putting him to bed.

"It's only a quarter to four," said Mimi.

There was a pause.

"I guess there's time," Skip said finally.

"I could go for a root beer," Buzzy added.

They stood up and walked down the porch steps. Her mind running away with her as usual, Kitty wondered if this was her first date. Buzzy fell in step with Mimi. Since the sidewalk was only wide enough for two, she and Skip were forced to walk side by side behind them. How could Mimi put her in a position like this! Whether Skip liked it or not, he had to walk with her! She tried to think of something to say, but her mind was blank. They walked two whole blocks with Mimi chattering away at Buzzy while Kitty tried to think of something to say. Apparently, Skip didn't mind, or else he couldn't think of anything to say, either. He walked along beside her with his hands in his pockets, jingling nickels and dimes, kicking an occasional pebble. Kitty noticed out of the side of her eye that Skip was very handsome. He had black, curly hair and brown eyes. His face was friendly, and he had a dimple when he smiled.

"What school do you go to?" said Kitty, startled at the sound of her voice.

"Central," said Skip quickly.

Silence again. They seemed to be back where they'd started.

Since Mimi had already told the boys Kitty was a friend from St. Joan's, Kitty could hardly tell him again where she went to school.

"What grade are you in?" she ventured at last.

"Ninth," he replied. "A freshman."

"Oh, so am I!"

Skip nodded. "Where do you live?"

Good grief! He was asking *her* something. He wanted to know where she lived. This seemed like a good sign.

"In Highland Park. On the other side of town."

"You're a long way from home."

Kitty wished she could think of a clever answer to that. She thought and thought, but her mind was blank again.

"I guess I am," she said, attempting an easy, casual laugh. "I'd never been to the east side until I met Mimi."

By now they had come to the root beer stand, and Mimi began giggling and punching Buzzy on the arm. She acted silly around boys, thought Kitty.

They all ordered root beers, and then Kitty suddenly remembered she didn't have any money with her. She whispered to Mimi but Mimi just whispered back, "Don't worry." She didn't volunteer to pay.

"Twenty cents," said the girl behind the counter.

At that point, Mimi spilled some root beer down the front of her sweater, and while she was making a big fuss about wiping it off, the boys reached into their pockets and paid for the root beers.

"I'm sorry," said Kitty, turning to Skip. "I didn't bring any money, but I'll pay you back."

"Forget it," he said. "It's on me."

"Well, thank you," said Kitty, embarrassed. It was the first time a boy had bought her anything.

Mimi had recovered from the root beer spill and was now busy drinking out of Buzzy's glass. "Half of mine got spilled," she said in a little-girl whine. She was standing on tiptoes to reach Buzzy's glass.

"Hey," said Skip, finishing his root beer. "I've got to go."

"I do too," said Buzzy. "I have to be home at five."

They all walked back as far as Buzzy's block, where the boys said goodbye. After they had gone, Mimi asked, "Do you think Buzzy likes me?"

Kitty didn't know what to say. She couldn't tell if he did or he didn't.

When Kitty didn't answer, Mimi said confidentially, "I think Skip likes you."

"Really?" said Kitty. "Why?"

"Well, did you notice how he walked with you? And how he paid for your root beer?"

"There wasn't anyplace else to walk," said Kitty, although she truly wanted to believe it was his choice. "And we didn't have any money, either of us."

"Doesn't matter," said Mimi. "Boys are supposed to pay, but they don't always, unless they like you. I'll bet he calls you."

On the streetcar ride home, Kitty settled down into the straw seat for the long ride across the open fields of St. Paul. She thought about the possibility of Skip's calling her. After all, he had asked where she lived. And he had bought her a root beer and said she didn't have to pay him back. He seemed like a kind, generous boy. And he was very handsome. But Kitty knew better than to count her chickens before they had hatched. She'd done that before. She would try to think of other things. But all the way home, and even that night in bed, all she could think about was Skip.

6
Getting
Ready

Despite the fact that Kitty had made up her mind to forget about Skip, the next day she found herself telling Eileen and Margaret Mary about him. And though she hated herself for it, she couldn't help exaggerating. "We were together all afternoon," she told them. "He asked me to go to the root beer stand with him." Then she added that he was tall, dark, and looked like the Greek god Apollo, who was pictured in their history book. The more she talked, the more convinced she became that he liked her and would call.

"Is he really as handsome as that Greek god?" demanded Eileen.

"Yes," said Kitty. "He's very, very handsome."

"Looks are not important," said Margaret Mary firmly. "Beauty is only skin deep."

Kitty had had enough of Margaret Mary's prim ways. Kitty decided she was probably jealous. "I like boys who are handsome," she insisted.

"Me too. I wouldn't want a boyfriend who wasn't handsome," said Eileen.

For a moment Margaret Mary seemed taken aback. Then she said stiffly, "Is he Catholic? I'd never go out with a boy that wasn't Catholic."

"Well, I would," said Eileen.

"I don't know what he is," Kitty admitted. "He goes to Central High, though."

Margaret Mary frowned. Central High was a public school.

"Did he say he'd call you?" asked Eileen.

"Well, he may as well have," said Kitty. "He asked where I lived, and we talked a lot . . . Then he bought me a root beer and we had lots of fun monkeying around at the root beer stand."

Margaret Mary and Eileen looked at her, a new respect dawning in their eyes. Who ever would have thought that Kitty would be the first one to date? It put her in a new light, and Kitty liked the way it felt.

"Of course," she said, "I won't see him too often. He lives way on the other side of the city."

Still, a boyfriend was a coup, even if he did live on the other side of the city and you never saw him. Kitty was sure she looked different now that she had a boyfriend. She felt happier and lighter, and she put on lipstick every morning, even though she had to take it off when she got to school. She combed her hair over one eye every day and not just when she went to Mimi's. She thought about Skip so much that pretty soon she couldn't remember what was real and what she had made up. She couldn't even remember exactly what he looked like. In her mind, he grew more and more handsome and more and more generous every day.

Kitty paid less and less attention to her schoolwork. In Latin class she found her mind wandering, and when Sister called on her to read, she often didn't know the place.

"Katherine," said Sister Sylvania sternly one day, "I will see you after class."

After class Sister lectured Kitty about her wandering mind and gave her extra homework.

In geometry class Kitty drew Skip's face in all the triangles in her textbook. In history she gave all the Greek gods black curly hair and brown eyes. And at home, her father was concerned because her report card had arrived in the mail and showed that her grades had fallen.

Kitty wished that Mimi would suggest walking by Buzzy's house again. Or better yet, Skip's house. She wasn't brave enough to lure boys alone. And part of her worried that the real Skip and the Skip in her mind were two different people.

Every morning Eileen would ask, "Did he call you?" Every day in geometry Mimi would say, "Did he call you?" Soon Kitty got tired of saying, "No, not yet."

Finally she said crossly to all of them, "I'll tell you if he does."

But as the days went on, he didn't. Mimi said that Buzzy had called her twice. Kitty wasn't sure she believed Mimi. She remembered how silly Mimi acted around boys. She recalled how giggly she had been the day at the root beer stand, and how she had said Buzzy liked her when Kitty could see no evidence that he did. It was terrible not to believe a friend, but Kitty had an uncomfortable feeling that Mimi might lie. Especially about boys. Of course, Buzzy *could* have called her. Mimi did know how to lure boys. There was no doubt about that.

And now, at school, everyone was talking

about the freshman prom, which would be held late in the fall. A committee had been formed to decorate the gym, and Kitty thought it would be fun to sign up for that. She couldn't persuade her friends to join her, though. Margaret Mary was on the committee to choose the band, and Eileen insisted she didn't like committees and wouldn't sign up for any at all. When Margaret Mary said she lacked school spirit, Eileen replied angrily that she didn't care and might not go to the prom anyway.

"Everyone goes to the prom!" Margaret Mary insisted. It was true. Everyone did go to the prom. It was a terrible thing not to go.

Sister Chrysostom called a special meeting of the freshmen to review courtesy and behavior at the prom. Dresses were to have long sleeves and high necklines. They should not be made out of revealing material, nor should they fit too tightly.

"Can we wear taffeta, Sister Chrysostom?" asked Margaret Mary.

"Yes, Margaret Mary, if it is not too shiny, and is of a color that is in good taste."

Margaret Mary's mother was planning to make her prom dress, and her parents were going to be chaperones for the event. They believed strongly in participating in school and community life.

Kitty loved all the commotion and discussion over the prom dresses, but she was afraid to allow herself to think too much about such things because she still didn't have a date. Everyone Kitty talked to had one or at least knew who they were going to ask. Kitty knew who she *wanted* to ask, but though she had convinced her friends that Skip liked her, she had not really convinced herself. She had not seen him since that day at Buzzy's house, and he had not called. Surely, if he really liked her, he would have called her by now.

Kitty did not want to be pushy and forward like other girls who everyone said were boy-crazy. Still, she did need a date for the prom. She could picture herself dancing with Skip.

(Did he know how to dance? she wondered.) She saw him, bright and handsome in his tuxedo, coming to her door, meeting her parents, shaking her father's hand. She saw him give her a corsage, maybe even an orchid. (Every girl at St. Joan's Academy wanted an orchid for the prom.) She saw him open the car door (what car? Skip was only a freshman—he wasn't old enough to drive, was he?) for her, carefully tuck her long dress in, close the door, and go around to the other side and get in himself. Kitty would sit close to Skip, she decided, but not too close. Not so close that he would think she was boy-crazy. She could smell his shaving lotion. (Did Skip shave?) Kitty frowned. She realized there was an awful lot she didn't know about him.

After the prom he would walk her to her front door. He would have his arm around her. Here Kitty was afraid even to dream that he would kiss her good night, although being kissed good night was the most important part of the evening. Kitty was sure that Mimi would kiss Buzzy good night, but her imagination stopped short of picturing herself kissing Skip. Well, it wasn't a kiss she needed to worry about yet, it was just a simple date for the prom.

"Who are you going with?" Kitty asked Eileen on the way home from school one day. Kitty was pretty sure Eileen intended to go to the prom. She just pretended to be uninterested to rankle Margaret Mary. Kitty knew how she felt — she often found herself wanting to take exactly the opposite stand from Margaret Mary.

"Oh, Robert, I suppose," said Eileen, sounding bored. Robert lived next door to her, his parents were friends of her parents, and he had gone to St. Anthony's with the girls. Sometimes he went to the movies with them on Sundays. He certainly couldn't be considered a boyfriend, he was too much like a brother. But at times like this, Robert came in very handy.

Margaret Mary, Kitty knew, was going with

a friend of her brother's. Although her mother said the girls were too young to date, she had made an exception for a school function that had the approval of the nuns.

As the days passed, Eileen and Margaret Mary became totally wrapped up in planning the evening. They talked about the latest dance steps and where to go after the dance. Kitty began to feel left out.

In geometry one day, Mimi said she was going to ask Buzzy. "Maybe we can double," she said.

Now Kitty felt awful. Kitty suddenly realized that she might end up decorating the gym — blow up hundreds of balloons and ruffle yards of crepe paper — without ever attending the dance.

"I don't have anyone to go with," said Kitty. "I mean, I'd like to ask Skip, but he hasn't called me . . ."

Mimi waved her hand through the air as if to dismiss that. "What's the difference?" she said. "You just have to lure him some more."

Kitty wasn't at all sure that would work. "I'm not as good at that as you are," she said.

On the streetcar the next morning, Margaret Mary and Eileen were talking about their prom dresses.

"My mom and I are going downtown to The Golden Rule this afternoon to get mine," said Eileen. "If they don't have what we want, we are going to the bridal shop on St. Peter Street. What are you going to wear, Kitty?"

"I don't think I'm going," said Kitty.

The two girls looked alarmed. They hadn't given much thought to Kitty's plight until now. All of a sudden it seemed serious.

"But aren't you going to ask Skip?" said Margaret Mary. "You said he liked you."

"But he hasn't called me," said Kitty. "I hardly know him." Kitty realized as she said this out loud that it was the truth. She hadn't believed it until now. She felt embarrassed admitting that she had exaggerated, but somehow she knew that her friends would forgive her.

Eileen and Margaret Mary didn't say anything about Kitty's previous exaggerations.

"Maybe he's shy," said Margaret Mary. "A lot of boys are."

"Why don't you ask him anyway?" said Eileen. "Maybe he'll say yes."

"Maybe I will," said Kitty, without much enthusiasm.

Every morning after that, the girls asked Kitty if she had asked Skip, and every morning Kitty said no. Finally the prom was only a week away.

"I'll do it tonight," she said to Eileen and Margaret Mary.

"Let's call him from my house," said Eileen supportively.

After school, the girls took the streetcar right to Eileen's house. Kitty's hands grew sweaty as they all looked up Skip's number in the telephone directory.

"Here it is," said Margaret Mary. "Dale 8257. Here, I'll give the operator the number."

"Dale 8257," said Margaret Mary clearly to the operator. "It's ringing," she said, her hand over the mouthpiece.

Kitty took the phone, wishing she had never heard of a prom. Or even of St. Joan's, for that matter. It wasn't as much fun as she had thought, going to high school. She was sure now that Skip would not even remember who she was.

"Hello," said a woman's voice.

"May I please speak to Skip?" said Kitty.

"One moment, please," said the voice.

"It's his mother," Kitty said to Eileen and Margaret Mary, covering the mouthpiece with her hand. She prayed that he wouldn't come to the phone. Maybe he was out. But she could hear his mother calling him. And she could hear his little brother whining in the background.

"Hello," said a boy's voice suddenly.

"Skip?" said Kitty, in a shaking voice. "Skip, this is Kitty. I don't know if you remember me, but you bought me a root beer a while back at the root beer stand, and I wonder if you would like to go to the prom at St. Joan's with me next Friday evening at eight o'clock." She said this all in one breath.

Margaret Mary and Eileen were nodding on with bright, encouraging eyes. They sat breathlessly waiting to hear his reply.

"Oh, really?" Kitty was saying. "Yes, yes, of course. Well, thank you, Skip. Goodbye." Kitty hung up the phone.

"Is he going, is he going?" shouted Eileen.

"I will never call a boy again the whole rest of my life," said Kitty.

"What did he *say?*" asked Margaret Mary. "Tell us."

"He said," Kitty spoke the words slowly, "that he would like to go with me."

Eileen and Margaret Mary whooped for joy.

"But," added Kitty, "he can't."

"Why not?" said Margaret Mary. "Does he have to take care of his little brother? Is he sick or something?"

"No," said Kitty. "He was already asked to the prom by someone else."

"By *who?*" said Eileen.

"By Mimi," said Kitty, on the edge of tears.

7
A Date for
the Prom

"*Mimi!*" said Eileen. "You said she was going with Buzzy."

"She was. At least, that's what she told me," said Kitty.

"What a low-down trick, to take someone else's boyfriend," said Eileen.

"He wasn't my boyfriend," said Kitty.

"Well, it wasn't very kind of Mimi," said Margaret Mary, who rarely said anything negative about anyone.

"That's just what an east-sider would do," said Eileen.

"I just can't believe it," said Margaret Mary.

The girls sat in silence, Kitty wiping her eyes with her hanky every few minutes.

"Well," said Eileen, finally, standing up. "It doesn't matter about him. What we have to do is think of someone who would want to go with Kitty."

"Yes," said Margaret Mary, putting her arm around Kitty. "That's the main thing. Eileen is right. You need a date. There has to be *someone* who would want to go with you."

Kitty was beginning to feel like one of the orphans at St. Joseph's Home on Randolph Avenue, the place that her mother and father sent Christmas baskets to every year. A charity case.

"Think," said Eileen. "Isn't there some boy you know? Even a boy you don't know. You could have a blind date."

The girls ran down the list of every boy they knew or had ever heard of. It didn't take long because there weren't many. There were no boys at St. Joan's, of course, and they hadn't seen any of the boys from St. Anthony's for a long time. Eileen said she wished Robert had a brother, and Margaret Mary said she could ask her brother if he had any friends she didn't know about.

"No," said Kitty. "I don't want to go with someone I never met."

"Well, we've run out of boys that you know, and you have to go the prom. You just have to. We all have to go together or it won't be any fun."

Kitty thought of herself sitting home alone in her room listening to her white radio, having supper with her mother and father, perhaps even studying her Latin, while Eileen and Margaret Mary were dancing, without her, in the colorful gym she had decorated. Afterward, they would go out to eat, laughing and joking with their dates. For weeks to come, all the girls would be talking about the prom, and Kitty wouldn't be part of it. This was definitely worse than being in the middle. Now she would be an outsider. She simply had to go to the prom.

"I'll think of someone," she said with more confidence than she felt, wondering who in the world it might be. She got her things together and walked with Margaret Mary as far as Jefferson Avenue and then said goodbye. As she walked up Jefferson, she gradually stopped feeling so sad and began to feel angry with Mimi instead. Wasn't one boy enough for her? Kitty only *knew* one boy, why did Mimi have to take him? Margaret Mary or Eileen would never do a thing like that, she fumed.

Kitty went to sleep that night angrily planning what she would say to Mimi in the morning.

But the next morning in geometry, Mimi would not look at her. She came in late and spent a good deal of time sharpening a pencil in the back of the room. When she took her seat, she seem particularly interested in what Sister Cleone was saying about the hypotenuse of a triangle. She waved her hand to answer a question.

"Mimi," whispered Kitty, loudly enough so Mimi would be sure to hear, "why did you ask Skip to the prom?"

Mimi's face flushed. She looked embarrassed and eager to explain. "Buzzy is going with someone else, so I had to ask Skip. I didn't think you were going to ask him, you were taking so long."

"Who else would I ask?" Kitty's anger was growing. New friends were difficult to understand. You never knew what they might do.

Mimi looked contrite. "I'm sorry!" she blurted out. "I didn't know who else to ask, and I just had to ask someone."

Why, of all things, Kitty suddenly realized. Mimi is as desperate as I am! She doesn't have any boyfriends either. Mimi, who knows how to flirt, who isn't nervous around boys. Mimi, the expert on luring boys. Kitty could hardly believe it. She wasn't the only one who had trouble finding a date for the prom. Mimi would have been in the same position she was in, if Kitty had gotten to Skip a few days earlier. Realizing this, Kitty's anger began to subside a bit. After all, she had to admit that Skip wasn't her own private property just because he had bought her a root beer.

Mimi was chattering apologies now, trying to make amends. "We'll have to lure some more boys right after the prom," she was saying.

"I have to lure one *before* the prom," said Kitty. "I simply have to go to that dance."

Two more days went by and none of the girls could think of anyone Kitty could ask. Then one day, as Kitty was riding with Eileen and Margaret Mary on the streetcar, she said, "My mother has an idea."

"Yes?" said her two friends eagerly. "What is it — tell us."

"She said I should ask my cousin Dickie." Kitty didn't look too enthusiastic at this prospect.

"Hurray!" said Eileen.

"That's a very good idea," said Margaret Mary warmly.

"I don't want to go with my cousin," said Kitty.

"Of course not, but he's a boy, isn't he? And it's better than not going at all," said Eileen, who was a realist. "You better ask him soon, the prom is in two days."

"My mom is going to ask my Aunt Marie when she talks to her on the phone," said Kitty. "She'll ask her today. If he does go," she added, "don't tell *anyone* he's my cousin."

The girls agreed not to tell.

When Kitty got to geometry she told Mimi about the plan. Mimi looked very relieved that Kitty was going after all. She crossed her heart to keep the secret about Dickie being her cousin. "Maybe we can double," she said. "You and Dickie and Skip and me."

"That would be fun," Kitty said, without thinking, and then she remembered that she had said she'd go with Eileen and Margaret

Mary. Besides, how could she face Skip after being turned down by him? Now Kitty had a new worry. As soon as one problem was solved, it seemed that another one came along to take its place.

When she saw Eileen and Margaret Mary at lunch, Kitty asked, "Are you two doubling for the prom?"

Eileen looked surprised. "We'll triple, you and me and Margaret Mary."

"Why, sure," said Kitty. She felt herself in the middle again. Mimi wanted to go with her, and Eileen and Margaret Mary wanted her to go with them.

"Why did you ask if we were doubling?" demanded Margaret Mary.

"I just wondered," said Kitty. "I hate to leave Mimi out. She has no one to double with." There. She had said the truth without beating around the bush. For the first time she had gotten out of a jam without waiting until there was big trouble.

"Honestly! After the rotten way Mimi

treated you, she deserves to go alone," said Eileen.

"She wasn't very nice, asking Skip behind your back," even Margaret Mary had to admit.

"She's sorry now," said Kitty. "She didn't know what to do when Buzzy turned her down. After all, I don't *own* Skip." Kitty couldn't believe that she was defending Mimi. But she couldn't seem to stay angry with her.

"I know what, then," said Eileen, softening some. "She can meet us there and we can all get together afterward. We'll just ride in different cars."

"We don't even have a car," said Kitty, worried. "My cousin doesn't drive."

"Neither does Aloysius," said Margaret Mary.

"Robert does," said Eileen. "He's sixteen," she added. "He can get his father's car for the night."

Kitty was impressed. This was really going

to be an exciting evening. They would actually be riding in a car with no adults.

But when she got home, and her mother said that Dickie could go with her, Kitty began to get depressed all over again. She thought of what fun all the other girls would have dressing up for the boys they were taking. She had heard that couples held hands in the car after they were out of the nuns' sight. That was not something you did with your cousin. And your cousin didn't bring you a corsage, much less an orchid. A cousin was someone you grew up with, and played in the sandbox with, and spent every birthday and Christmas with since you were a baby. A cousin was something like a brother, often just barely tolerated. She hoped the girls would remember not to tell anyone that Dickie was her cousin.

Worst of all, the gossip after the prom, she knew, would center on who had been kissed and who hadn't. A kiss from a cousin was simply no kiss at all.

"I thought you'd be happy about Dickie," her mother said.

"I am," sighed Kitty, trying to cheer up. Maybe Eileen was right. It may not be fun going to a prom with your cousin, but it was better than not going at all.

8
The Prom

Her mother didn't have time to sew a prom dress, so Kitty, without much enthusiasm, went shopping for one. Mimi had volunteered to lend her one of her sister's formals, but Kitty was pretty sure that a dress of Fluffy's would not be suitable for an SJA prom.

She finally found a light-blue organdy dress with a peter pan collar and long sleeves. Her mother liked it because it was practical. After the prom it would be shortened and hemmed to make a fine dress for church on Sundays. Since she couldn't expect her cousin to bring her a corsage, Kitty decided to wear a bunch of fresh flowers at the neck.

On the eve of the prom, Mimi called Kitty

with a new problem. "Skip's father can't drive us," she said. "Something is wrong with his car. We have no way to get there."

Into Kitty's mind came a dreadful picture of the four of them taking the streetcar to the prom, the girls' long dresses trailing up and down the dirty car steps. After all, she couldn't let Mimi take the streetcar alone.

"What will we do?" said Mimi. "We've simply got to have a car."

"I'll check with Eileen and call you back."

When Kitty explained their plight, Eileen said, "We'll all have to go in one car."

"We'll be too many, won't we? What will your parents say?"

"They won't mind. They think Robert is very responsible. Besides — we don't have to tell them."

"Will we all fit?"

"We can sit on laps and stuff. We'll squeeze."

"What fun!" said Mimi, when Kitty told her. "We'll quadruple! Eileen and you and

Robert in the front seat, and your cousin and Skip and me and Margaret Mary and Al in the back!"

Kitty wished Mimi would not always refer to Dickie as her cousin. And here she already had the seating arrangement worked out. No doubt she was looking forward to being squeezed in with Skip and two other boys in the back seat. Kitty had a sudden suspicion that Mimi might even have made up the story about the ailing car.

"Well, I guess it's the best we can do," she said grudgingly. She did not relish the notion of sitting in the front with Eileen and Robert.

"I think it sounds like a lot more fun than taking two cars," said Mimi.

In spite of herself, Kitty was looking forward to the dance. It would be fun to see everyone out of uniform and in long dresses. She started getting ready early the day of the prom and was ready by 7:30. At eight o'clock Dickie came to the door (his father had brought him) in his best suit. Kitty recognized it from family parties. He seemed to think that going to a dance with his cousin was the most natural thing in the world. He had a fresh crew cut for the occasion. Kitty hadn't noticed before how lanky he was — all arms and legs and smile. He seemed to have grown since Christmas.

"Hi," said Dickie cheerfully. "I don't know how to dance too well."

"I don't either," admitted Kitty nervously. She had always assumed you just follow the boy, who is supposed to lead and should know what he is doing. But after coming this far, she was not about to let a little thing like not knowing how to dance too well stand in the way of this prom. "Just move your feet back and forth," she said. "It doesn't look hard."

Dickie smiled. How they managed on the dance floor was obviously not going to worry him one bit. Kitty would have to do all the worrying for both of them, it seemed. She sighed. It wasn't going to be an easy evening.

Kitty's mother insisted on taking a picture of Kitty and Dickie on the front lawn, despite

Kitty's protests and Dickie's grinning face. She was about to take another one when, mercifully, Eileen and Robert drove up. Abiding by Mimi's seating arrangement, Kitty and Dickie climbed into the car. They waved goodbye to Kitty's mother, then stopped to pick up Margaret Mary and Aloysius before they started for the east side to get Mimi and Skip.

Margaret Mary's homemade dress was pink taffeta with long sleeves and a high neck like Kitty's. At her shoulder, she wore a corsage — of pink roses and baby's breath — from Aloysius. Eileen's dress was a beige, princess-style one with three-quarter length sleeves and a not-so-high neck.

"It's shantung," said Eileen. She had a corsage of daisies and chrysanthemums tied to her wrist and was wearing her new high heels and her Cyclamen Evening lipstick. She looked much older and more worldly than Margaret Mary and Kitty.

But when they picked up Mimi and Skip, Kitty had to admit that Mimi was definitely the most worldly among them. She was wearing a long dark satin dress with sequins that sparkled when she moved. It had a neckline that was even lower than Eileen's, and there was an orchid pinned to the waist. The first thing she did when she got into the car was to explain how the sleeves of her dress were only snapped on. She demonstrated by removing them and putting them in her purse.

"Look," she said.

The girls turned to see Mimi's bare arms and a good bit of her bare neckline. Kitty was shocked, but Eileen only said, "I wish I'd thought of that."

"That is against regulations," said Margaret Mary.

"No, it isn't. See, presto, I'll just snap them right back on when we get there," said Mimi, bouncing up and down on Skip's lap. "And afterward, poof, I'll take them off when we leave." Mimi snapped her fingers.

Margaret Mary argued. "I think Sister

meant the regulations were for the whole evening, not just for school."

"They can't tell us what to wear when we're out of school," said Mimi. Eileen agreed, and that started a long, heated discussion among the three of them.

Oh dear, thought Kitty, the evening was getting off to a bad start. The boys, who did not know each other, were quiet all the way to school.

Kitty had been nervous about seeing Skip again. He did not look a bit as she remembered him, except for the black curly hair and the dimple. The tuxedo gave him a very dignified appearance, and as soon as Kitty saw him, she knew she liked him better than ever. Eileen whispered to Kitty, "He *is* as handsome as you said!" And Kitty was surprised to find she had not exaggerated his looks.

When they arrived, Kitty looked out the car window at all the girls walking in their bright formals, arm in arm with their dates, and felt a sudden urge to jump out of the car and run home. But by now Dickie had crawled out of the back seat, straightened his trousers, and was offering his elbow to her with a big smile on his face. Well, at least *he* didn't feel awkward about being with his cousin.

As they walked into the gymnasium, Mimi sidled up to Kitty and whispered, "Your cousin is *cute!*" Then she winked at Kitty.

Could Mimi be serious? Kitty was astounded. She never thought of her cousin as someone a girl would take seriously. As a boyfriend, anyway.

Kitty entered the room surprised at the hundreds and hundreds of brightly colored balloons bobbing overhead, even though she had helped to hang them. Tables were set up along the walls and held vases of chrysanthemums and asters, as well as bowls of candies, nuts, and punch. She could hardly believe this was her school, it was so festive. The band was tuning up in one corner. The nuns, all in black, seemed out of place as they milled about. Everyone's face was rosy, flushed with excitement. One boy was pinning flowers on a girl's dress, another was polishing his shoes with a hanky. Kitty realized she had never seen the school after dark. With the bright lights coming through the crepe-paper streamers, it looked different from the daytime gym full of white-suited girls playing volley-ball.

Dickie asked Kitty to dance. As she stepped out onto the floor with him, she could feel several eyes on her. Casting a quick look over her shoulder, she saw that many of the girls were staring at her date with admiration. She realized happily that the only ones who knew that Dickie was her cousin were Eileen and Margaret Mary and Mimi.

She felt a tap on her shoulder.

"May I cut in?"

Skip wanted to dance with her! Kitty's head began to reel until she saw Mimi sliding into Dickie's arms. She remembered how Mimi had winked. It was probably Mimi who wanted to cut in, not Skip. Good heavens, Mimi had already taken Skip away from her, and now she was stealing her cousin. Not that Kitty really minded losing her own cousin, but it did prove Mimi could not be trusted around boys. Kitty felt angry with Mimi all over again.

"I'm sorry I couldn't take you to the prom," Skip said, looking at her very seriously. "But it looks like you didn't have any trouble finding someone to go with." He seemed hurt.

If only she had admitted right at the beginning that Dickie was her cousin. It was probably too late to tell Skip now. She'd sound as bad as Mimi.

As they danced around the floor (it was getting easier all the time), Ruthie Cobza brushed by Kitty and whispered, "Who is that guy you came with? I've never seen him around before. He's a dreamboat."

Before Kitty could reply, Skip swept her off across the room in a waltz. She felt like she was floating. What a fine dance this was.

After that number ended, Mimi came to re-trieve Skip, and Kitty danced in turn with Robert and Aloysius and then with Dickie again. While she was with Dickie, three other couples cut in and exchanged partners. "Where did you meet him?" asked one of the girls.

Kitty had to think fast. "Our families have known each other for a long time," she said honestly.

Looking over at Dickie, she saw that he was definitely having a good time. He was sur-rounded by a group of girls who were clapping as he did a new Lindy step for them.

"Where did you learn that?" she said when he came back to her.

"I just made it up," he said.

Kitty took a long look at her cousin. She was beginning to think she had underestimated Dickie all these years. She remembered how clever he had always been. When they were little, he had made cardboard furniture for her dolls without a pattern. It shouldn't come as a surprise that he could make up dance steps, but Kitty had never pictured Dickie as a person apart from the family at holidays.

"Where are we going afterwards?" said Mimi, dancing up to Kitty. Before Kitty could answer, Mimi said, "I think we should go out of town."

"Out of town?" echoed Kitty. "I don't know . . . Robert is driving."

"Here they are now, we'll ask him," said Mimi.

The band was in the middle of a long drum solo, but Kitty saw Robert and Eileen nod after Mimi said something to them. "A good idea," Kitty heard Eileen say.

A wave of alarm swept over her. Why couldn't Margaret Mary's Aloysius have driven? He would never drive out of town in the middle of the night. There was no end of things that could happen. Well, surely Margaret Mary would discourage this idea. She would know better than to go out of town. No doubt her mother would expect her to come home right after the dance. After all, her parents were chaperones.

But when Kitty ran into Margaret Mary on the dance floor, all she said was, "Eileen and Robert and Mimi and Skip want to go somewhere out of town. That should be fun, don't you think?" Then, as if answering Kitty's unasked question, she added, "I just asked my mother. She said that school dances are special nights, and she trusts me not to do anything foolish. So I don't have to be in early or anything." Margaret Mary danced away with Aloysius's arm tightly around her, and looked as if she was enjoying it immensely.

Margaret Mary's mother trusted her not to be foolish. Well, going out of town was certainly foolish. Kitty had been sure that Margaret Mary could be relied on, if anyone could, and now not even she was acting like herself. Here she was, willing to drive out of town in the middle of the night, on lonely country roads, tempting fate — as Sister Chrysostom would say — by putting herself in the path of temptation. What was happening to everyone tonight?

9
The Spiral Bridge

At midnight the band played the last dance number, "Blue Skies," which was the prom theme song. The girls had rehearsed the song together in classroom meetings, and Sister Chrysostom had changed the line, "When you're in love, my how they fly by," to "When times are right, my how they fly," saying it was more fitting for young ladies at St. Joan's Academy. Now, however, Kitty heard Eileen singing "When you're in love" right out loud.

"Blue days," sang Kitty, "all of them gone, nothing but blue skies, from now on." She swayed to the music. As Margaret Mary danced by, she noticed her dancing cheek-to-cheek with her date, which was forbidden. The lights were low, though, and the chaperones, including her own parents, probably weren't noticing.

When the dance was over, the crowd poured out through the doors, many of the couples arm in arm and still singing. The first thing Mimi did, as soon as the group gathered together, was to tear the sleeves off her dress and throw them into a rubbish barrel. "Good riddance," she said, her bare white skin showing in the moonlight.

While Mimi was dismantling her sleeves, Kitty had gotten into the back seat of the car. "It's someone else's turn to sit in front now," she said, though she knew full well that Mimi was the only one still standing outside. Margaret Mary and Aloysius were sitting cozily in one corner of the back seat, and Kitty settled down between Skip and Dickie. No one looked ready to move. Mimi stood outside with her hands on her hips and her bottom lip out, pouting. "Well, I'm not going to sit up in front all alone," she said, stamping her foot.

Skip made no move to get out. Finally Dickie volunteered to sit in front. "Mimi can sit on my lap," he said. He untangled his long arms and legs and climbed into the front seat. Mimi squealed as she got in after him.

Now, with four in the front seat, there was more room in the back seat. Skip slipped his arm around the back of the seat, and it slowly settled around Kitty, just as if she were his date. In the front seat Dickie was saying something to Mimi that was making her squeal even more than usual.

"Now," said Robert, turning around to all of them, "where should we go?"

"I hear Hastings is fun," said Mimi. "We can drive across the spiral bridge and go and eat at McNulty's."

"Hastings is twenty miles from here!" said Kitty.

"Great!" said Margaret Mary. "Let's go to Hastings!"

"Hastings it is," said Robert, starting the car.

Kitty gasped. Until tonight Margaret Mary had always been so dependable and careful. If she could act so strangely, anything could happen.

"Let's sing!" said Dickie, as the car hit the open road. He began by singing the first line of "Mairsy Doats," and pretty soon everyone was singing lustily, even Kitty.

"If the words sound queer,
and funny to your ear,
a little bit jumbled and jivey,
sing mares eat oats
and does eat oats
and little lambs eat ivy."

When they finished that, Eileen suggested "South of the Border." The group picked up the tune quickly. "That's where I fell in love, when stars above come out to play," Skip sang loudly.

Kitty got goose bumps all over. It almost felt like he was singing to her. No boy had ever sung to her before. And certainly not a love song.

"And that's where I wander, my thoughts ever stray . . . south of the border, down Mexico way . . ."

Kitty saw that Aloysius was singing into Margaret Mary's ear, and Dickie was singing to Mimi. The only one not singing was Robert, and that was probably because he was driving.

As they rode on, singing and joking, the conversation turned to the nuns. Suddenly Kitty assumed the voice of Sister Sylvania, short and clipped. "Mimi, conjugate the verb *to be.*"

"I can't, Sister," squeaked Mimi. "Latin is a dumb dead language and I hate it."

"Ha," said Eileen. "Don't you wish you really could say that to Sister Sylvania?"

"Do some more nuns, Kitty," said Skip. "You really are funny."

Did he really think so? Well, she could be *very* funny if she tried.

Kitty mimicked Sister Chrysostom and Sister Cleone and even Father Bliss. The whole group was clapping now, Skip the loudest of all. And the more they clapped, the more Kitty play-acted. When she ran out of nuns at St. Joan's, she mimicked the nuns at St. Anthony's. And when she ran out of them, she began to recite the rules in "Courtesy Counts." The whole way to Hastings Kitty kept everyone entertained.

"You're a card, Kitty, do you know that?" said Margaret Mary, who just yesterday would have been scandalized by Kitty's behavior.

"You really are," said Skip, giving Kitty a little hug that sent more shivers down her spine.

"Are you cold?" asked Skip.

"A little," said Kitty, knowing that wasn't why she was shivering.

Skip took off the coat of his tuxedo and put it around her shoulders. It was still warm from his body, and it smelled of Aqua Velva, like the rest of him. Kitty was pretty sure she was imagining all of this — it couldn't be real. She would have pinched herself, but she didn't want to move and disturb Skip's arm, which was around her now.

"You know what, Kitty," whispered Skip. "You should be a comedian. On the radio. You've got a lot of talent."

Kitty didn't know which was more fun, having Skip like her or being the life of the party. She was surprised how much she liked being the center of attention. If so, why was she wasting her time in Latin class? She was a born showman. Or a show-off, she could hear her mother or Sister Chrysostom saying. Why was it their voices were always inside her head, answering her every thought? Well, even if she never did go to acting school or on the radio, the important thing was that Skip liked her. He thought she was funny, and that felt good.

The time had gone so fast, with Kitty's entertaining, that they were already in Hastings.

Looming ahead was the famous spiral bridge. The bridge arched in a long high loop from one shore to the other. From a low shore to a higher one. Underneath was a network of support, with metal steps to give repairmen access for maintenance.

"O-o-o-h," squealed Mimi. "Look how high it is!"

"It looks like a ride at the fair," said Dickie.

"Do you know what?" said Mimi, as they approached the bridge. "Some kids I know walked underneath it, on those steps. All the way across the river!" Mimi had some attention back now. It had been hard for her to give it up to Kitty.

"Fools," said Aloysius, who up to now had been very quiet. "You'd never catch me doing a crazy thing like that!"

"I don't know," said Margaret Mary. "It might be kind of fun."

"Ha!" said Mimi. "You'd be the last one to do a thing like that."

"I might," said Margaret Mary.

"Not you," repeated Mimi. "You're such a goody-goody."

A pained look passed over Margaret Mary's face.

"I dare you," continued Mimi, with fire in her eyes. "I dare you to walk across the river underneath that bridge."

Margaret Mary's face was red and her jaw was set. She looked angry and frightened. By now Robert had come to a halt at the stop sign before the bridge. Hesitating for only a moment, she jumped out and was over the guard rail and on her way before anyone could stop her.

"A goody-goody, am I!" Margaret Mary meant to shout, but her voice was only a whisper.

"Come back here! Margaret Mary, come back here!"

"You'll be killed!" shouted Kitty. "Come back here right now!"

"We can't let her do it!" shouted Aloysius, running after her. But she was already far away. "Her brother will kill me if anything happens to her!" He started to follow her and then hesitated. "One of you guys come with me," he said.

"We could all be killed," said Robert uneasily. "As long as she's made up her mind, I think we should just drive across the bridge and meet her on the other side."

In the distance they could see Margaret Mary. She was following the steps underneath the bridge and holding on to the cables tightly as she went. As they started to drive across the bridge, she was directly underneath them.

"I don't believe this!" said Eileen, covering her eyes. "What got into Margaret Mary tonight?"

That was what everyone was thinking. What had gotten into Margaret Mary?

"That was a dumb thing to do, to dare her," Eileen said to Mimi.

"Well, I never thought she'd do it," said Mimi, whose face had turned white now. "She was always such a quiet girl. A real prude."

"She's no prude," said Robert quickly.

Everyone agreed. Margaret Mary was certainly no prude tonight.

Kitty had no idea what to think. She had read books about people like this. People who suddenly turned into someone else. But who would ever have expected such a sudden change in behavior from Margaret Mary? It just wasn't like her at all.

"Maybe," said Eileen, "you just can't be as good as Margaret Mary all your life without exploding once in a while." It sounded right. Margaret Mary was definitely exploding now.

Robert parked the car on the other side of the bridge, and they sat and waited for Margaret Mary. No one felt like singing now. Aloysius climbed across the guard rail so he would be the first one to meet her. Kitty sat huddled in Skip's coat and made up a little prayer, just as the nuns had taught them to do in a crisis. "Please God," prayed Kitty, "don't let anything happen to Margaret Mary. Let her get back here safely soon. Amen."

"She'll be all right," whispered Skip in Kitty's ear.

"I hope so," said Kitty.

"You have nice friends," he said. "I like them — and Dickie too," he added.

"He's my cousin," Kitty blurted out.

Skip didn't seem shocked. "He's a nice guy," was all he said.

Finally they saw Margaret Mary coming along the steps and up the shore. She had a big smile on her face. "I told you I could," she said to Mimi. "I did it!"

The welcoming group hooted and applauded as she came up the bank, not so much to congratulate her as to express the relief they felt. Kitty hugged Margaret Mary tightly and promised God never to criticize her or to talk about her to Mimi again.

"That was a crazy thing to do, you know," said Aloysius, who was perspiring heavily now. He was wiping his forehead with a large handkerchief.

When they all got back into the car, and Margaret Mary told about how scary it had been — how she had seen the water rushing underneath her — Mimi began to pout. Mimi did not like not being the life of the party. Kitty knew how she felt because a moment ago she had felt like that herself. It was strange. Although Mimi was proving not to be as perfect as Kitty had first believed, they had many things in common.

"Well, as my mother would say, 'all's well that ends well,' " laughed Margaret Mary.

Kitty couldn't believe her ears! After what she had just done, Margaret Mary was still quoting her mother.

Before too long, Robert was pulling into McNulty's. Feeling lighthearted again, the group piled into the high black booths. This time Skip bought Kitty not only a root beer, but two hamburgers and a hot fudge sundae besides. Mimi fed Dickie little pieces of her chili dog and talked baby talk, and Aloysius bought Margaret Mary some hot chocolate to warm her up after her dangerous ordeal. Robert even had his arm around Eileen.

After they finished eating, they were all suddenly very tired. The girls' flowers were wilting, and their dresses were dirty and frayed on the bottom, especially Margaret Mary's. They got up to go. Mimi began yawning as they piled back into the car, and she fell asleep on the way home.

By the time they got to Kitty's house, it was after midnight. Her father had been waiting up for her (she could tell because through the window she could see him reading in the living room). But the light went out as soon as she put her key in the lock, and by the time she had opened the door and walked into the house, he was in bed.

Skip walked up to the door and came into the living room with her. "Just to be sure you're safe," he said. And then, of all things in the world, he leaned over and kissed her on the cheek. She debated whether she should kiss him back, but it seemed forward and she didn't want to be pushy. It was enough that Skip, who was not even her real date, had kissed her.

She, Kitty, had been kissed by a boy. She had thought if this ever happened she would want to get to school quickly and tell everyone about it. Or call her friends on the phone to compare notes. But instead, she was surprised to find that she wanted to hug the moment to herself, a small warm secret that was very private.

"I'll call you," Skip said as he left.

Kitty knew he would.

She closed the door and leaned against it. Skip liked her. She had been herself, just plain Kitty, and Skip liked her. She had never had such a good time in her whole entire life. Perhaps that was what Margaret Mary had discovered tonight, too, when she exploded — that people could like you, even if you weren't perfect all the time.

Kitty climbed into bed, weary and happy. Just before she fell asleep she had one final thought. She made up her mind to change the "i" back to "y" in her name and become Kitty again, permanently.